For Lois - her wisdom and guidance is my magic - L.C.
To Sheri and to my husband Maurice, who turned a fantasy into reality - J. H. H.

PUBLISHED BY RIP SQUEAK, INC.
840 CAPITOLIO WAY, SUITE B
SAN LUIS OBISPO, CALIFORNIA 93405

Library of Congress Control Number: 2008921878

ISBN-13: 978-1-934960-13-4

FIRST EDITION, FIRST PRINTING

Art Direction by Sheri Barnes
∼
Design by Willabel L. Tong

Don't miss the other books in this series:
RIP SQUEAK AND HIS FRIENDS ∼ THE TREASURE ∼ THE ADVENTURE

To learn more about other products from Rip Squeak, visit
www.RipSqueak.com

PRINTED IN CHINA

A RIP SQUEAK® BOOK
Find the Magic

Written by **Lee Cohen**

Illustrated by **Julia Harnett Harvey**

Based on characters created by
Susan Yost-Filgate and Leonard Filgate

RIP SQUEAK, INC. ∽ SAN LUIS OBISPO, CALIFORNIA

ONE BRIGHT and shiny morning, Euripides the frog arrived at the cottage to visit his friends.

"I'm stuck," Rip Squeak admitted as soon as he saw Euripides. "I just can't figure out what to draw."

"Hmm," said Euripides thoughtfully, "We will have to find a solution."

Rip's little sister, Jesse was struggling to dress her doll, Bunny, as a fairy princess.

"I absolutely cannot get these costumes to look right," Jesse sighed. "I'm getting very impatient and so is Bunny!"

"My, my, my," mused Euripides, scratching his head and looking very concerned.

Just then, Abbey the kitten came around the corner. "There is not one nook or cranny that I have not explored a hundred times," said Abbey. "As everyone knows, cats are naturally curious and there's nothing even remotely curious about this house."

"Oh, dear," sighed Euripides. "We will have to figure out what to do about all of this."

The clever amphibian was never without a plan. If he didn't have a plan, at least he had an idea. If he didn't have an idea, at least he had a thought or two.

"Perhaps we can…" he muttered. "No, no – that won't work," he added, interrupting himself. "Maybe we can… no, that isn't quite right, either." Then, as if a great idea had just dropped right into his lap, he announced dramatically, "I have it! I will take you all to a magical place!"

Rip, Jesse and Abbey looked up from their doldrums. They were ready to follow Euripides.

"We've been walking a very long time," sighed Rip and indeed, they had. They had walked past the cottage grounds, away from the pond and along the old country road.

"Never fear," roared Euripides. "We're almost to the magic place."

They finally reached a little shop where they pushed and pushed on a heavy door until it was open but a smidgen – which, by the way, is just enough room to let a frog, a cat and two little mice through.

Inside, the friends were greeted by a most unexpected sight. From floor to ceiling, there were shelves and shelves and more shelves crammed and jammed with books: big books, small books, little books, fat books, thin books. Books everywhere!

As Rip, Jesse and Abbey eyeballed their surroundings, Euripides exclaimed, "It's time you see for yourselves that there is magic all around us!"

He opened a large volume and waved Rip forward. "Spend a moment with this book," Euripides whispered. "Gaze deep into the picture, if you will, and find the magic…"

It was a book about knights in shining armor. Rip found himself caught up in the tales of the brave and bold warriors, their code of chivalry and their gallant deeds. He felt like he could step inside the very pages of the book.

And then he did.

When Rip finally looked up from the book, he smiled at Euripides. "Now I know exactly what to draw!" he said.

"But what about me?" begged Jesse.

"Take a look here," Euripides said as he opened another book and laid it before her. "This world of fantasy is all yours!"

Jesse turned to a picture of a fairy wonderland, filled with lovely flowers and gentle creatures. She couldn't take her eyes off the page and magically, she was transformed.

When Jesse closed the book, she could barely catch her breath. "Bunny will be so impressed when we play fairy princess. I'll make her the best costume ever!"

"*1001 Arabian Nights!* This looks worth exploring," Abbey said, as she crawled up onto the pages of a book. Almost immediately, she was transported.

When she finished reading, Abbey purred, "There's no reason for me to ever get bored again – not with so many incredible stories!"

Euripides sat back and watched his friends with their heads buried deep in their stories. Their earlier mood had vanished and they looked happy and content.

Then Rip was tugging on Euripides' jacket. "Euripides," he said, "You've been so busy finding magic for all of us – you haven't found any for yourself."

Abbey and Jesse nudged a book forward and Rip opened it. "Yes," he cried. "It's perfect for the friend who helped us figure out the answers to our problems and saved the day!"

Euripides looked at the book they had chosen for him and chuckled, "Why, this is just how I imagine myself!" He began to read aloud: " 'The thick London fog closed in around the great detective.' " In an instant, Euripides found himself a hundred years and a thousand miles away.

When Euripides was able to pull himself away from his story, he glanced at his pocket watch and announced that it was time to head back.

"But there's so much more to look at," said Rip.

"Of course," said Euripides. "There are books of high adventure and history, tales of fantasy and mystery, stories of far-off lands. But never fear, my friends.

"Anytime we need to learn or be inspired – or when we just want to have fun – the magic will always be here!"